THE USBORNE BOOK OF KITES

Susan Mayes

Kite consultant: Jeff Tearle

Designed by Carol Law

Illustrated by Angie Sage

Additional ideas by Ray Gibson

With special thanks to Margaret Greger and John Spendlove for the use of their "Square kite" design.

Contents

First published in 1992 by Usborne Publishing Ltd, Usborne House, 83-85 Saffron Hill, London EC1N 8RT, England. Copyright © Usborne Publishing Ltd, 1992.

The name Usborne and the device 🎈are Trade Marks of Usborne Publishing Ltd.

Getting ready

The first kites were made in China, about two and a half thousand years ago. This book shows you how to make a whole variety of colourful and exciting kites for yourself.

There are lots of decoration ideas plus tips on how to fly your finished models. To get the best results, make each kite as accurately as you can.

Things you will need

You can buy most of the things to make the kites in this book from newsagents, hobby shops or "do-it-yourself" shops. At the beginning of each project there is a list of all the things you will need.

Here are some useful tips to remember when you prepare some of your materials.

Kite maker's tips

1. Before you start, clear a big space and collect all the things you need. Always have these four things ready.

Long ruler

Pencil

Scissors

Stick of glue

2. Follow all the instructions very carefully.

3. Use the knots suggested in each project. They are strong, kite maker's knots.

4. Be patient when you fly your kite for the first time. It takes a little practice (see pages 12 and 13).

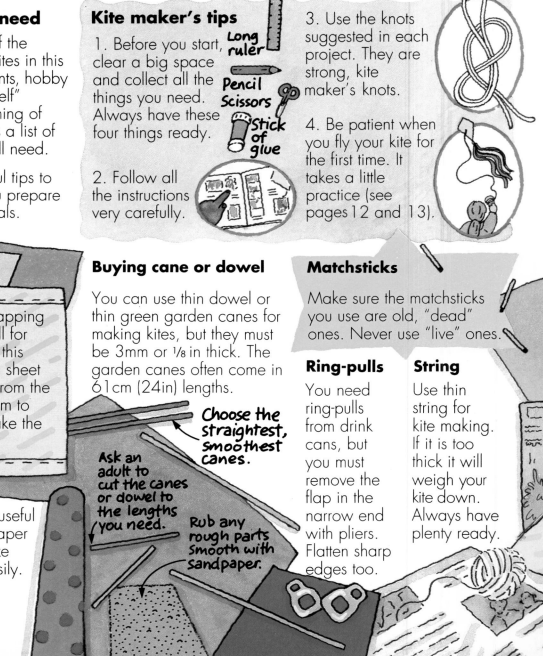

Buying paper

Some sheets of wrapping paper are too small for making the kites in this book. Buy an extra sheet and cut two strips from the long side. Stick them to the first sheet to make the size you need.

Rolls of paper are useful as you get more paper and can cut the size you need more easily.

Buying cane or dowel

You can use thin dowel or thin green garden canes for making kites, but they must be 3mm or ⅛in thick. The garden canes often come in 61cm (24in) lengths.

Choose the straightest, smoothest canes.

Ask an adult to cut the canes or dowel to the lengths you need.

Rub any rough parts smooth with sandpaper.

Matchsticks

Make sure the matchsticks you use are old, "dead" ones. Never use "live" ones.

Ring-pulls

You need ring-pulls from drink cans, but you must remove the flap in the narrow end with pliers. Flatten sharp edges too.

String

Use thin string for kite making. If it is too thick it will weigh your kite down. Always have plenty ready.

Parts of a kite

There are lots of different sorts of kites, but their parts have the same names. You will come across these words.

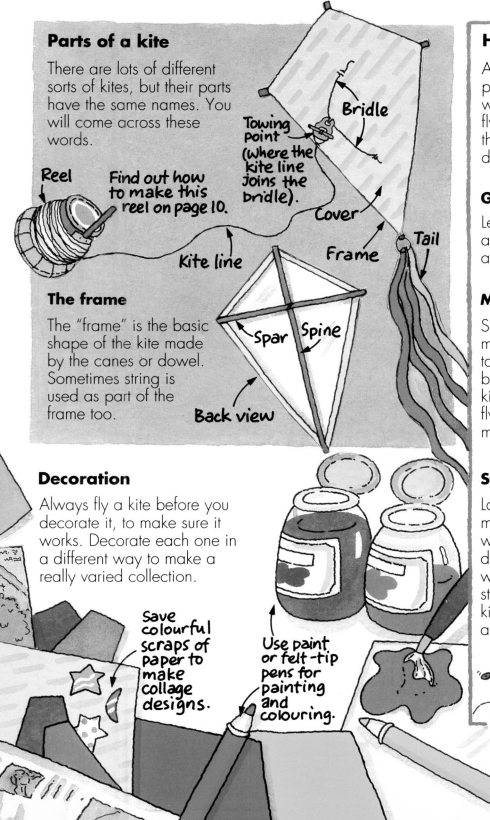

Reel

Find out how to make this reel on page 10.

Bridle

Towing point (where the kite line joins the bridle).

Cover

Tail

Frame

Kite line

Spar Spine

Back view

The frame

The "frame" is the basic shape of the kite made by the canes or dowel. Sometimes string is used as part of the frame too.

Decoration

Always fly a kite before you decorate it, to make sure it works. Decorate each one in a different way to make a really varied collection.

Save colourful scraps of paper to make collage designs.

Use paint or felt-tip pens for painting and colouring.

How windy is it?

At the beginning of each project you can find out what sort of wind is best for flying your finished kite. Use this guide to help you decide how windy it is.

Gentle wind

Leaves rustle and move about gently.

Moderate wind

Small branches move. A kite's tail blows out behind. Most kites in this book fly best in a moderate wind.

Strong wind

Large branches move. Walking with your kite is difficult. If the wind is too strong, your kite may crash and break.

3

Paperfold kite

Make this simple kite from any thin paper. It flies best in a very gentle wind.

You will need:

Three pieces of thin paper 21 x 29.5cm (8¼ x 11½in)

A thin drinking straw
Clear sticky tape
Cotton thread
A paperclip

Tip

Lay a ruler between the dots and fold the paper over it.

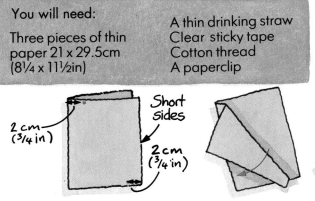

Short sides

2 cm (¾ in)

2 cm (¾ in)

1. Take one of the pieces of paper. Fold the short sides to meet each other. At the top, mark a dot 2cm (¾in) from the left corner. At the bottom, mark a dot 2cm (¾in) from the right corner.

2. Pull the top layer towards you and make a fold between the dots. Now turn the whole sheet of paper over. Fold the top piece towards you, so the crease matches the one underneath.

3. Unfold the top piece of paper again, then turn the whole sheet of paper over. Lay a ruler between the left and right corners and draw a pencil line across the paper, as shown above.

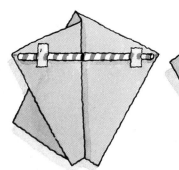

This folded part is called the keel.

Label this line A.

2.5cm (1in)

A

Label this line B.

A

4. Mark the straw's centre. Lay the straw along the line with the mark on the kite's centre fold. Put sticky tape on each side.

5. Turn the kite over. Lay a ruler between the left and right corners. Draw a line across the folded part only.

6. Mark a dot on the folded edge, 2.5cm (1in) above line A, as shown above.

7. Draw a line from the dot to the place where A meets the kite's centre fold.

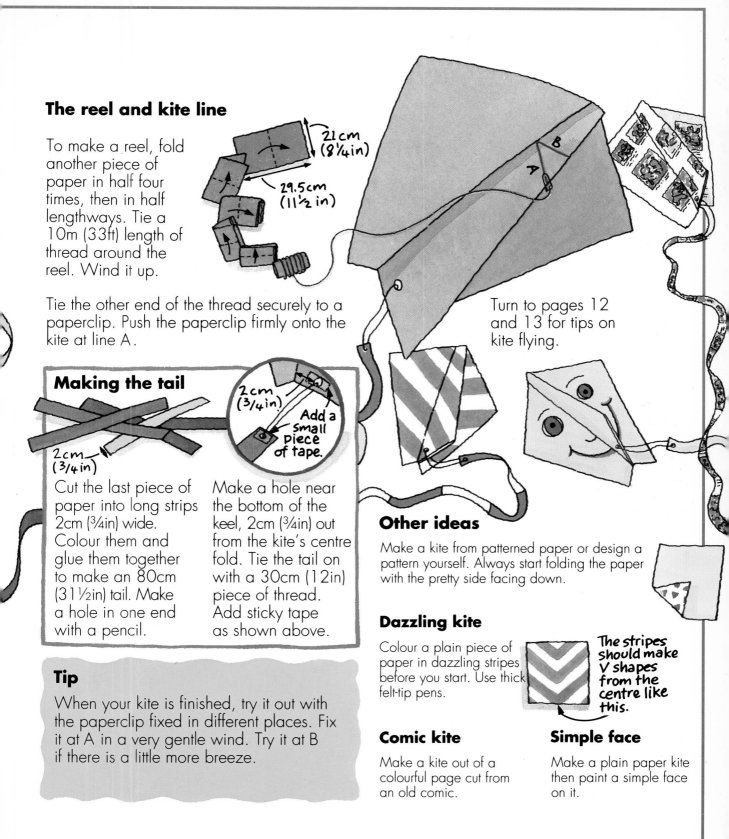

The reel and kite line

To make a reel, fold another piece of paper in half four times, then in half lengthways. Tie a 10m (33ft) length of thread around the reel. Wind it up.

21cm (8¼in)

29.5cm (11½in)

Tie the other end of the thread securely to a paperclip. Push the paperclip firmly onto the kite at line A.

Making the tail

2cm (¾in)

Add a small piece of tape.

2cm (¾in)

Cut the last piece of paper into long strips 2cm (¾in) wide. Colour them and glue them together to make an 80cm (31½in) tail. Make a hole in one end with a pencil.

Make a hole near the bottom of the keel, 2cm (¾in) out from the kite's centre fold. Tie the tail on with a 30cm (12in) piece of thread. Add sticky tape as shown above.

Tip

When your kite is finished, try it out with the paperclip fixed in different places. Fix it at A in a very gentle wind. Try it at B if there is a little more breeze.

Turn to pages 12 and 13 for tips on kite flying.

Other ideas

Make a kite from patterned paper or design a pattern yourself. Always start folding the paper with the pretty side facing down.

Dazzling kite

Colour a plain piece of paper in dazzling stripes before you start. Use thick felt-tip pens.

The stripes should make V shapes from the centre like this.

Comic kite

Make a kite out of a colourful page cut from an old comic.

Simple face

Make a plain paper kite then paint a simple face on it.

Flat diamond kite

This traditional European kite flies best in light to moderate winds. You can find out how to make it on the next six pages.

There is a lot to do, but it is worth it in the end. You will use some of these steps to help you make other kites too.

You need these things to make the frame and cover:	Patterned wrapping paper, brown wrapping paper or newspaper 56 x 61cm (22 x 24in)	Two 60cm (23½in) lengths of thin cane or dowel (3mm or ⅛in thick) Thin string

Tip

Hold the paper down to help you cut both layers.

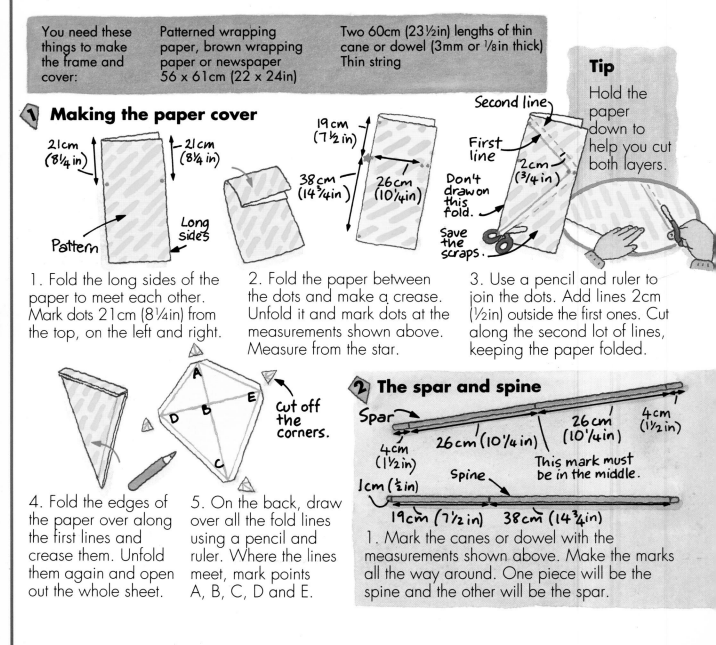

① Making the paper cover

21cm (8¼ in) — 21cm (8¼ in)

Pattern — Long sides

1. Fold the long sides of the paper to meet each other. Mark dots 21cm (8¼in) from the top, on the left and right.

19cm (7½in) · 38cm (14¾in) · 26cm (10¼in)

2. Fold the paper between the dots and make a crease. Unfold it and mark dots at the measurements shown above. Measure from the star.

Second line · First line · 2cm (¾ in) · Don't draw on this fold. · Save the scraps.

3. Use a pencil and ruler to join the dots. Add lines 2cm (½in) outside the first ones. Cut along the second lot of lines, keeping the paper folded.

A · E · B · D · C · Cut off the corners.

4. Fold the edges of the paper over along the first lines and crease them. Unfold them again and open out the whole sheet.

5. On the back, draw over all the fold lines using a pencil and ruler. Where the lines meet, mark points A, B, C, D and E.

② The spar and spine

Spar · 4cm (1½in) · 26cm (10¼in) · 26cm (10¼in) · 4cm (1½in) · This mark must be in the middle.

Spine · 1cm (½in) · 19cm (7½in) · 38cm (14¾in)

1. Mark the canes or dowel with the measurements shown above. Make the marks all the way around. One piece will be the spine and the other will be the spar.

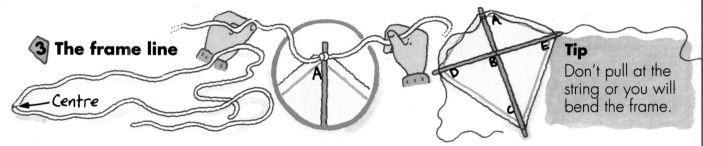

3 The frame line

Centre

Tip
Don't pull at the string or you will bend the frame.

1. Cut a piece of string four times the length of the spine. Fold it in half and make a mark at the centre.

2. Glue around the spine at A. Tie the string on tightly with its centre mark at A. Add more glue around the knot.

3. Glue along edges A to D and A to E. Lay one piece of string in each crease. Fold the edges over. Press them down.

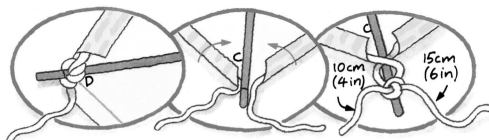

10cm (4in)   15cm (6in)

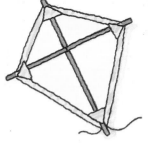

4. Glue around the spar at D. Tie a knot at the corner to keep the string secure. Now do the same at E.

5. Glue the other two edges. Lay the rest of the string in the creases and fold the edges over.

6. Glue the spine at C. Cross the strings over the top, then under and over again. Tie a double knot. Add glue. Trim the ends as shown.

7. Cut triangles from the leftover scraps of paper. Stick them over the corners of the kite, to add extra strength.

The 1cm (½in) mark is over point A.

The second mark is over point B.

Spine

The middle mark is over the spine.

Spar

Gap

2. On the cover, glue along the line from A to C. Glue one side of the spine and stick it along line A to C. Press it down and let it dry.

3. Put glue along the line from D to E. Glue along one side of the spar and stick it to the paper along line D to E. Press it down. Let it dry.

Tip
Don't try to make the cover stick to the spar where it crosses the spine. There should be a small gap.

4. When the glue is dry, fold the edges of the cover in and crease them along the lines. Then unfold them again.

The bridle

You will need these things:

A 120cm (47½in) piece of thin string threaded onto a thick needle
A spare piece of string (about 30cm (12in) long)
A ring-pull from a drink can (save the can)

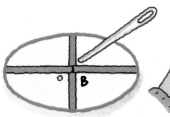

1. Use the needle to make two holes close to B. Make them in opposite corners of the cross made by the spar and spine.

2. Practise the knot on the right using a pencil and the spare string. In the next step you will tie the knot on the kite itself.

Round turn with two half hitches

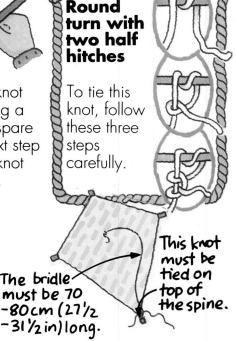

To tie this knot, follow these three steps carefully.

The bridle must be 70 -80cm (27½ -31½in) long.

This knot must be tied on top of the spine.

3. With the spar and spine facing upwards, poke the threaded needle up through one hole and down through the other one. Do this again. Turn the kite over.

4. Unthread the needle and adjust the string so one end sticks out about 10cm (4in). Now tie the rest of the knot. Gently push it down to the kite's face.

10cm (4in)

5. Put some glue around the bottom of the spine. Tie the long end of the string around it using another round turn with two half hitches.

Tip

Hold the bridle as shown above to check that the kite is balanced. If it goes down on one side, put pieces of sticky tape on the other side, to balance it.

Adjust the position of the ring-pull in different winds (see page 12).

6. Tie the ring-pull to the bridle about 25cm (10in) from the centre of the kite. Use the lark's head hitch on the right.

The lark's head hitch

Double the string. Poke it through the ring-pull from behind.

Slip the loop over the top of the ring-pull.

Now pull the knot tight.

5 The tail

You will need these things:

Coloured tissue paper
A 15cm (6in) piece of thin string
A matchstick
A thick needle

1. Choose coloured tissue paper to match your kite. Cut it into strips measuring about 3cm (1¼in) wide. Glue the strips together to make four streamers, each measuring 4m (13ft) in length.

2. When the glue is dry, crush each streamer into a ball. Gently smooth each one out again. Do this a second time. You must crush the streamers like this or your kite will not fly properly.

3. Glue 9cm (3½in) at one end of each streamer. Fold the ends over 3cm (1¼in) then fold them over again. Glue the corners and fold them in. Add pieces of sticky tape.

4. When the glue is dry, use a needle to make a small hole in each folded end. Thread the streamers onto the 15cm (6in) piece of string. Tie the ends of the string in a reef knot.

Reef knot

① ②

5. Now tie the ends of the kite's framing string (page 7) in a reef knot.

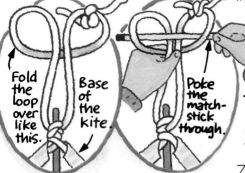

Fold the loop over like this.

Base of the kite.

Poke the matchstick through.

6. Tie the framing string onto a matchstick with a lark's head hitch as shown above.

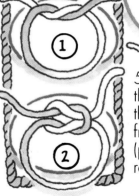

The loops for the new knot go around the outside.

The first knot you made is in the middle.

7. Tie the tail string onto the same matchstick with another lark's head hitch.

Tip

If it is quite windy your kite will fly better with an extra tail streamer. If there is less wind, take one of the streamers off. It is easy to undo the knots to make changes.

6 The reel and kite line

You will need these things:

An empty drink can
Thick dowel, 20cm (8in) long and 8mm (1/3)
A matchstick
Thin string, 60m (196ft)*
A piece of thick cardboard
Something circular
Sandpaper

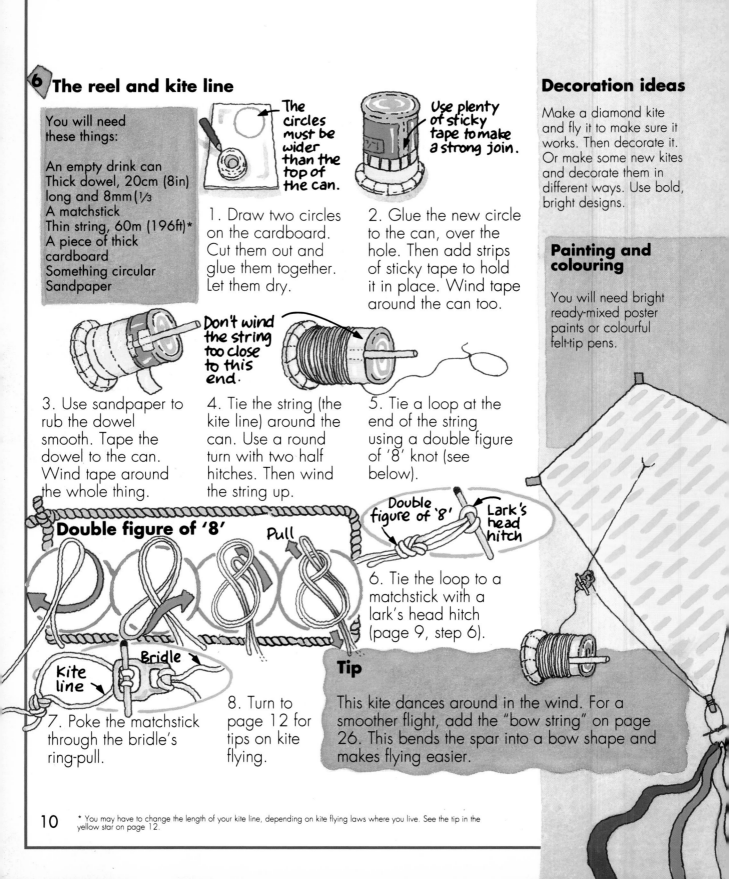

The circles must be wider than the top of the can.

Use plenty of sticky tape to make a strong join.

1. Draw two circles on the cardboard. Cut them out and glue them together. Let them dry.

2. Glue the new circle to the can, over the hole. Then add strips of sticky tape to hold it in place. Wind tape around the can too.

Don't wind the string too close to this end.

3. Use sandpaper to rub the dowel smooth. Tape the dowel to the can. Wind tape around the whole thing.

4. Tie the string (the kite line) around the can. Use a round turn with two half hitches. Then wind the string up.

5. Tie a loop at the end of the string using a double figure of '8' knot (see below).

Double figure of '8'

Pull

Double figure of '8'   Lark's head hitch

6. Tie the loop to a matchstick with a lark's head hitch (page 9, step 6).

Kite line   Bridle

7. Poke the matchstick through the bridle's ring-pull.

8. Turn to page 12 for tips on kite flying.

Tip

This kite dances around in the wind. For a smoother flight, add the "bow string" on page 26. This bends the spar into a bow shape and makes flying easier.

Decoration ideas

Make a diamond kite and fly it to make sure it works. Then decorate it. Or make some new kites and decorate them in different ways. Use bold, bright designs.

Painting and colouring

You will need bright ready-mixed poster paints or colourful felt-tip pens.

* You may have to change the length of your kite line, depending on kite flying laws where you live. See the tip in the yellow star on page 12.

Collage

You will need scraps of brightly coloured tissue paper or coloured self-adhesive film.

Make a white paper kite. Cut bold shapes from the tissue paper or self-adhesive film. (Don't use thick paper.) Stick them on before you add the kite's bridle and tail.

Overlap different coloured shapes.

The shapes can overlap on to the back of the kite.

Try out some ideas on rough paper first. Then paint your favourite design on to a plain paper kite before adding the bridle and the tail. Add black outlines to help pick out the shapes.

You could glue tissue paper shapes to the ends of the streamers.

Tip

Check that your kite is balanced (see page 8). If it isn't add more shapes to the higher side.

More tail ideas

You will need coloured tissue paper and 4m (13ft) of string.

Flag tail

22cm (8½ in)

18cm (7 in)

Cut off these corners.

Cut triangles from tissue paper. Fold it first, so you can cut lots at once.

Glue the triangles to the string as shown above.

Tie a double figure of '8' knot (page 10) at one end of the string. Tie the tail to your kite (page 9, steps 6 and 7).

Bow tail

Cut strips of tissue paper, 3 x 12cm (1¾in x 4¼in). Then tie them tightly to the string every 10cm (4in). Attach the tail, as above.

You will need about 40 bows.

Tip

Don't make your paint too watery. If you do, the paper will get soggy and the colour won't be very strong.

Changing the shape

You will need stiff paper.

Work out a design which uses pairs of paper shapes to change the kite's outline. Stick the shapes on before you paint your design.

Add hands which stick out.

Add feet.

Try out some different sorts of tails.

Tip

Always stick the shapes on the left and right sides of your kite, to make sure it is balanced. Don't make them stick out too far.

Flying your kite

Here are some tips to help you fly your kite safely and successfully, whatever size and shape it is. Take a friend to help you practise - it's more fun.

Where to fly

The best places to fly kites are open spaces such as fields and uncrowded beaches. If you fly your kite on a hillside, stand where the wind blows uphill, from behind you.

The wind is too blustery on this side.

Keep away from buildings and trees. The wind blows around them in gusts and makes flying difficult.

Things to take

When you go kite flying, take these extra things with you:

Gloves to stop the line from cutting into your hands.

Sticky tape for on-the-spot repairs.

Tails of different lengths and extra tail streamers.

DON'T

- fly your kite near roads or overhead cables.

- fly your kite in a thunderstorm.

DO

Contact an airport to find out about special kite flying laws. For instance, in the United Kingdom you must not fly kites above 60m (196ft) or within 5km (3 miles) of an airfield.

Tip

Most of the kites in this book fly best in moderate winds (see page 3). If the wind is too weak or too strong, wait for better kite flying weather.

Test the towing point

By moving the ring-pull (the towing point) up or down the bridle you can change the way your kite faces the wind. When the kite is at the correct angle, the wind will move smoothly past it and lift it high into the air.

1. Hold the bridle loosely at the ring-pull. If the kite catches the wind and is fairly steady, the ring-pull is in about the right place.

2. If the bridle slips through your fingers, move the ring-pull to the place where the bridle rests in your hand.

Try the ring-pull here.

Tip

Try moving the ring-pull up the bridle in stronger winds. Try moving it down the bridle in weaker winds.

Launching your kite

1. Check all the knots before you launch your kite or you may lose it.

2. Ask your helper to hold the kite up as shown. It must face into the wind.

3. Stand with your back to the wind. Let out about 5m (16ft) of line. Try not to tug at the kite.

4. When you are ready, tell your helper to push the kite up. Slowly let out more line.

5. If the kite starts to fall, tug the line gently. As the kite rises again, let out more line.

Tip

If your kite starts to dive and spin, or will not climb, you may need to adjust the bridle or even the tail. See the last section on this page for extra tips.

Flying alone

Stand with the wind behind you. Hold the kite by its towing point, so it faces into the wind. Let out a little line with the other hand. Release the kite gently into the air.

Bringing your kite down

Bring your kite down carefully. Wind the line slowly around the reel, or ask your helper to pull the line down for you, while you wind it up.

Making adjustments

If you have followed the intructions on these pages and your kite still won't fly very well, try making these adjustments.

1. The bridle

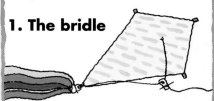

Most problems can be solved by moving the bridle's ring-pull. Move it 2cm (¾in) at a time, to find the right towing point.

2. The tail

Some kites need a tail to steady them as they fly and climb. It drags behind and helps keep the kite's face lifted into the wind.

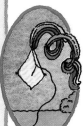

If your kite dives and spins, its tail may be too short. Add another streamer or try a longer tail.

If your kite won't climb, its tail may be too long. Remove a streamer or try a shorter tail.

Dragon kite

This is one of the most spectacular kites in this book but it is also quite tricky to make. You will need a friend to help you. Find out how to make and decorate the dragon on the next six pages. There are some different decoration ideas on page 19. Fly your finished kite in moderate to fairly strong winds.

You will need these things:

Crêpe paper 60 x 60cm (23½ x 23½in) or two pieces of tissue paper 60 x 60cm (23½ x 23½in) stuck together with blobs of glue

Nine pieces of brightly coloured crêpe paper or tissue paper 30 x 70cm (12 x 27½in) for the tail

Three pieces of thin cane or dowel (3mm or ⅛in thick): 30cm (12in), 50cm (19½in) and 60cm (23½in)

Thin string
A ring-pull
A thick needle

Tip

If you use dowel, soak the longest piece in water overnight. It will be easier to bend in section 1.

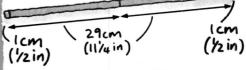

Making the bow

1cm (½in) 29cm (11¼in) 1cm (½in)

1. Mark the 60cm (23½in) piece of cane or dowel with the measurements shown above. Make the marks all the way around.

1cm (½in) mark

2. Tie an 80cm (31½in) piece of string close to one end. Use a round turn with two half hitches (see page 8).

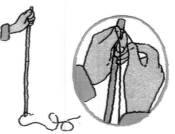

3. Stand the cane or dowel on the end with the knot. Hold it as shown above. Take the string up over your thumb nail and around the cane or dowel.

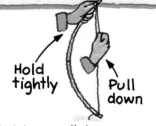

2 Adding the spine and spar

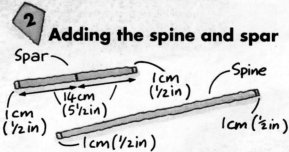

Spar

1cm (½ in)

14cm (5½ in)

1cm (½ in)

1cm (½ in)

Spine

1cm (½ in)

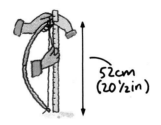

Hold tightly

Pull down

4. Now pull the string down gently to make the wood bend into a bow shape. Your thumb will stop the string from slipping down the bow.

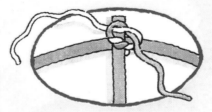

52cm (20½ in)

5. Ask your helper to measure the distance between the ends of the bow. Stop pulling the string when the ends of the bow are 52cm (20½ in) apart.

Trim the end.

This is the bow string. It must measure 52cm (20½ in).

6. Ask your helper to hold the bow. Tie the string on close to the end using a round turn with two half hitches. Glue both knots.

1. Mark the other canes or pieces of dowel with the measurements shown above. The short piece will be the spar. The long piece will be the spine.

3. Lay a 30cm (12in) piece of string under the cross made by the bow and spine. Bring the ends over to the top, so they cross the bow and spine. Then tie them in a double knot.

5. Trim the ends of the string and add glue all around the join. Let it dry.

2. Ask your helper to lay the spine on the bow so that one 1cm (½ in) mark matches the bow's centre mark. She must hold the bow and spine while you do steps 3, 4 and 5.

4. Now cross the ends of the string over the bow and spine the other way. Take them underneath, then bring them over to the top again. Tie them in a double knot.

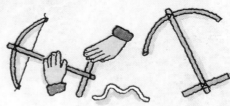

6. Ask your helper to lay the spar under the spine so that the spar's centre mark matches the spine's other 1cm (½ in) mark. Add string and glue as you did in steps 3, 4 and 5.

③ Adding the cover

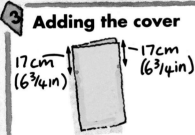

17cm (6¾in)   17cm (6¾in)

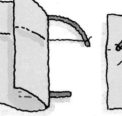

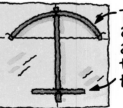

The bow and spar are on top of the spine.

1. Fold the crêpe paper or tissue paper in half. Measure and mark 17cm (6¾in) from the top at both sides, as shown above.

2. Fold the paper over between the dots. Press along all the folds. Then unfold the whole piece of paper.

3. Lay the frame with the spine facing upwards. Glue along the spine between the 1cm (½in) marks.

4. Turn the frame over. Match the spine with the paper's centre fold. Match the bow string with the other fold. Stick the frame down.

5. Turn the frame over. Lift the left side of the paper. Glue along the bow and spar from their 1cm (½in) marks right up to the paper.

6. Lower the paper, making sure that the bow string matches the fold line. The spar must lie straight too. Press the paper so that it sticks firmly to the frame.

7. Now glue the right side in the same way. Let it dry then turn the whole thing over.

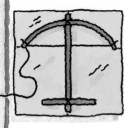

Tip

Don't pull the string too tight. It will pull the frame out of shape.

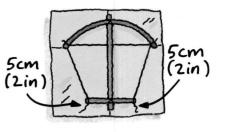

5cm (2in)   5cm (2in)

8. Cut a 60cm (23½in) piece of string. Tie one end to the left end of the bow with a double knot. Take the string down to the spar's left end and tie it on with another double knot. Glue around both knots.

9. Tie a 60cm (23½in) piece of string to the right side of the frame using the method in step 8. Trim the string at the bottom to 5cm (2in).

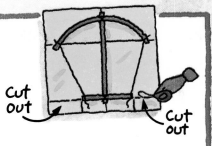

A **The bridle**

10. Draw straight lines from the ends of the spar to the bottom of the paper and from the ends of the spar to the sides of the paper.

11. Now cut out the rectangles at the bottom of the paper, on the left and right sides.

cut out

Cut out

1. With the frame facing upwards, use the needle to make a hole in the paper at the top of the spine, to the right. Thread 220cm (86in) of string onto the needle.

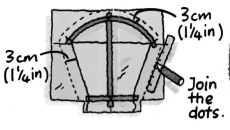

3cm (1¼in)

3cm (1¼in)

Join the dots.

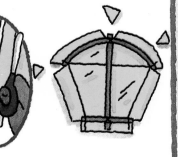

2. To tie the string on using a round turn with two half hitches, first poke the needle up through the hole. Take it across the spine and bow, over to the other side of the kite.

12. Mark dots 3cm (1¼in) out from the framing string and the bow. Join the dots at the sides with a pencil and ruler. Join the ones on top by eye.

13. Cut along the lines you have just drawn. Then cut out triangles at the places shown above.

3. Now do the same again, then turn the kite over.

The string is in the crease.

4. Unthread the needle and tie the rest of the knot (see step 4 on page 8).

14. Glue along the cover's left edge. Fold it over the string and stick it down. Do the same on the right edge.

15. Snip the paper around the bow every 2cm (¾in). Glue each piece and stick it down over the bow.

17

10cm (4in)

This must measure at least 180cm (7lin).

5. Mark the spine 10cm (4in) up from the spar. Make holes in the cover on each side. Tie the end of the string through the holes using a round turn with two half hitches (see page 8). Glue the knots.

Tip

Check that your kite is balanced and make any adjustments (see the tip on page 8).

6. Measure the bridle to find its centre. Tie the ring-pull 10cm (4in) above the centre using a lark's head hitch (see page 8).

7. To make the reel and kite line, turn to page 10, or use one you have made already.

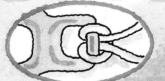

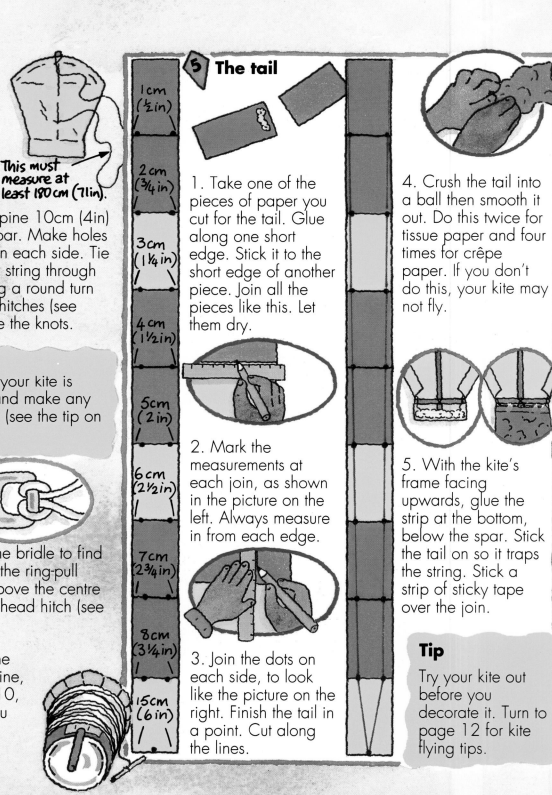

5 The tail

1. Take one of the pieces of paper you cut for the tail. Glue along one short edge. Stick it to the short edge of another piece. Join all the pieces like this. Let them dry.

2. Mark the measurements at each join, as shown in the picture on the left. Always measure in from each edge.

3. Join the dots on each side, to look like the picture on the right. Finish the tail in a point. Cut along the lines.

1cm (½in)
2cm (¾in)
3cm (1¼in)
4cm (1½in)
5cm (2in)
6cm (2½in)
7cm (2¾in)
8cm (3¼in)
15cm (6in)

4. Crush the tail into a ball then smooth it out. Do this twice for tissue paper and four times for crêpe paper. If you don't do this, your kite may not fly.

5. With the kite's frame facing upwards, glue the strip at the bottom, below the spar. Stick the tail on so it traps the string. Stick a strip of sticky tape over the join.

Tip

Try your kite out before you decorate it. Turn to page 12 for kite flying tips.

Decoration ideas

You can decorate your kite to look like a dragon, or you could make it into something completely different. Sketch out some rough ideas first.

Make a dragon or a serpent by sticking colourful paper shapes on the head and tail.

Flying cupcake

Use bright scraps of paper and thick felt-tip pens to decorate the flying cupcake.

Tissue paper flowers

Felt-tip lines to make a tablecloth.

Tip

You must crush the tail twice after decorating it, to soften the extra paper.

Super spook

Add black paper shapes to a white kite to make this super spook.

Spooky paper features

Try a paper chain at the end of the tail.

Felt-tip hands. You could draw around your own.

Mermaid

Make a kite with a yellow top and a green tail. Add bright decorations to make it into a mermaid.

Paper shells and starfish

Felt-tip lines for hair

Add clam shells.

Draw felt tip scales, or use paint.

Add paper fins here.

Dracula

Make a black kite. Add purple paper to make the shape of Dracula's cloak. Add a head and hands.

Stick on hands made from stiff paper.

Stick on a purple cloak.

Tip

If you use paint, don't make it too watery.

19

Super silver kite

Make this kite from shiny silver wrapping paper which looks like foil. It will shimmer in the sunlight. Fly it in moderate winds.

You will need these things:

Silver wrapping paper which looks like foil 37.5 x 37.5c
Two pieces of thin cane or dowel (3mm or 1/8in thick): 53cm (29¾in) and 60cm (23½in)

Thin string
A thick needle
A ring-pull
Tissue paper (for the tail)
Clear sticky tape

Tip

If you choose patterned silver paper, start section 1 with the pattern facing down.

1 The cover and the frame

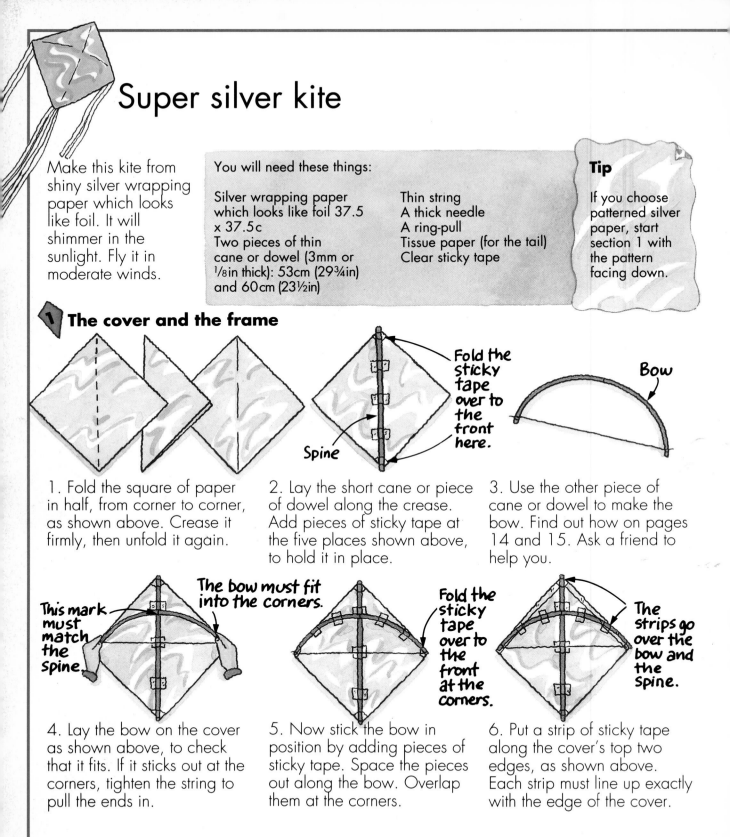

Fold the sticky tape over to the front here.

Spine

Bow

1. Fold the square of paper in half, from corner to corner, as shown above. Crease it firmly, then unfold it again.

2. Lay the short cane or piece of dowel along the crease. Add pieces of sticky tape at the five places shown above, to hold it in place.

3. Use the other piece of cane or dowel to make the bow. Find out how on pages 14 and 15. Ask a friend to help you.

This mark must match the spine.

The bow must fit into the corners.

Fold the sticky tape over to the front at the corners.

The strips go over the bow and the spine.

4. Lay the bow on the cover as shown above, to check that it fits. If it sticks out at the corners, tighten the string to pull the ends in.

5. Now stick the bow in position by adding pieces of sticky tape. Space the pieces out along the bow. Overlap them at the corners.

6. Put a strip of sticky tape along the cover's top two edges, as shown above. Each strip must line up exactly with the edge of the cover.

② The bridle

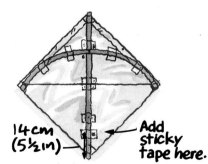

14cm (5½in)

Add sticky tape here.

1. Make holes in the cover, in opposite corners of the cross made by the bow and spine.

2. Mark the spine 14cm (5½in) from the bottom, then put sticky tape over that point. Make holes in the cover on either side of the mark.

This should measure about 80cm (31½in).

Add glue here.

3. Thread a 120cm (47¼in) piece of string onto the needle. Tie it through the top holes (see page 8, steps 2 to 4). Tie the other end through the bottom holes.

4. Tie the ring-pull about 35cm (13¾in) from the top end of the bridle using a lark's head hitch (see page 8). Attach the reel and kite line (see page 10).

③ Adding streamers

1. To make tissue paper tail streamers, see page 9, steps 1 and 2. For this kite you need four streamers, each measuring 5m (16½ft) long.

2. Glue 4cm (1½in) at one end of each streamer. Stick the streamers to the back of the kite, at the base. Add sticky tape too.

3. Now make four streamers which are 1.5cm (½in) wide and 1.5m (5ft) long. Stick two to each wing tip, then add sticky tape.

21

Birdie kite

You can find out how to make and decorate this birdie kite on the next six pages. You could even make some more and fly them in a flock, with your friends. The birdie flies best in moderate winds.

See how to make the birdie template on page 32.

You will need these things:

Plain paper 50 x 60cm (19½ x 23½in)
Crêpe paper 50 x 66cm (19½ x 26in) or two pieces of tissue paper 50 x 66cm (19½ x 26in)

Extra crêpe paper or tissue paper for the tail
Thin cane or dowel (3mm or ⅛in thick): 42cm (or 17in) and 60cm (23½in)
Thin string
A ring-pull
A thick drinking straw
A thick needle

1. Cutting out the cover

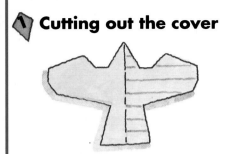

1. To make the shape of this kite, you need to draw a shape to cut around. This is called a template. See how to make the birdie template on page 32.

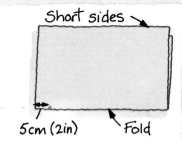

2. Fold the short sides of the crêpe paper, or one piece of tissue paper, to meet each other. Make a mark 5cm (2in) along the fold. Then unfold the paper.

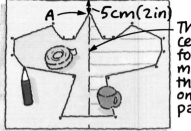

3. Lay the template on the paper with point A on the 5cm (2in) mark. Put heavy objects on it to keep it still. Mark dots on the paper at each corner as shown above.

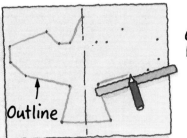

4. Remove the template. Use a pencil and ruler to join the dots as shown above. Draw carefully. Check that your shape looks like a bird.

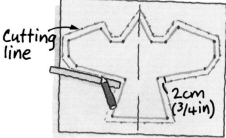

5. Mark dots 2cm (¾in) outside the outline. Join them using a pencil and ruler. This is the cutting line. Cut along it all the way around.

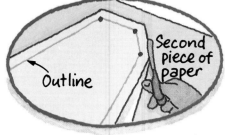

6. If you have used tissue paper, turn the birdie over. Glue along its edges and dot glue all over the shape. Stick it onto the second piece of paper then cut out the shape again, as shown above.

Making the frame

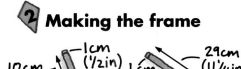

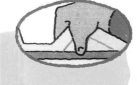

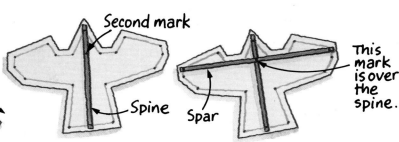

1. Mark the canes or dowel all the way around with the measurements shown above. The long piece will be the spar and the short piece will be the spine.

2. Glue the spine between the 1cm (½in) marks. With its second mark near the head, match the top mark with the tip of the pencil outline. Stick the spine to the centre fold.

3. Glue the spar between its 1cm (½in) marks. Match these marks with the outline's wing tips as shown above. Stick the spar down. Let it dry.

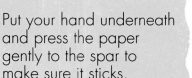

Tip

Put your hand underneath and press the paper gently to the spar to make sure it sticks.

4. Cut a 180cm (71in) piece of string. Fold it in half and mark the centre.

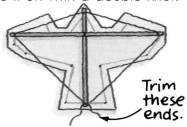

5. Glue around the 1cm (½in) mark on the spine, at the head end. Place the string with its centre under the mark. Tie it on with a double knot.

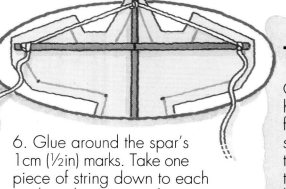

6. Glue around the spar's 1cm (½in) marks. Take one piece of string down to each mark and tie it on with a double knot.

Tip

Check that you have not pulled the frame out of shape. If you have, then the string is too tight. You must loosen it a little.

7. Glue around the 1cm (½in) mark at the bottom of the spine. Tie the pieces of string on one at a time with double knots. Glue all the knots.

23

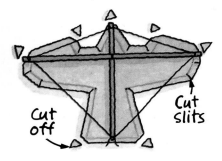

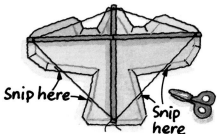

8. Cut off the seven corners shown above. At the other corners, cut slits up to the pencil outline.

9. Then snip into the lower edges where the string crosses them. Be careful not to cut the string itself.

10. Cut two strips of paper, each measuring 2 x 4cm (¾ x 1½in). Stick them close to the outline's corners at the top of the tail, as shown above.

11. Cut a 2.5m (8ft) piece of string. Fold it in half and mark the centre. Lay the mark under the spine, at the top. Tie the string on with a double knot.

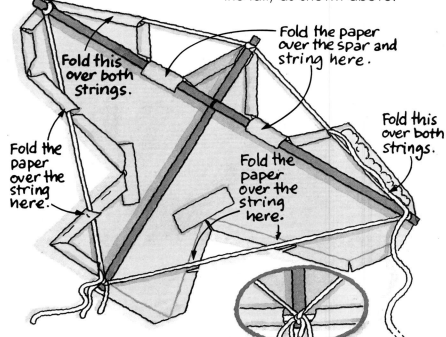

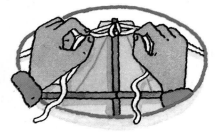

12. At the top of the kite, glue the first edge on the left. Lay one piece of string along the line. Fold the paper over the string and press it down.

13. Stick the string all around the birdie's left side using the method in step 12. Then stick the other piece of string all around the right side. The tips above will help you.

14. Glue around the base of the spine. Wind each piece of string around the spine once. Tie the ends together on top with a double knot, then trim them.

3 The bridle

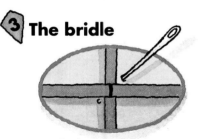

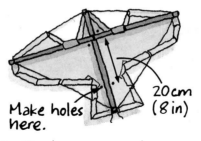

Make holes here.

20cm (8in)

1. With the frame facing upwards, use a thick needle to make two holes in the cover where the spar and spine cross. Make them in opposite corners.

2. On the spine, make a mark 20cm (8in) down from the cross made by the spar and spine. Then make holes in the cover on either side of the mark.

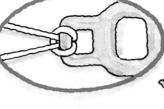

This should be about 60cm (23½in) long.

3. Thread a 100cm (39in) piece of string onto the needle. To tie it through the top holes, turn to page 8. Steps 2 to 4 show you how to tie a round turn with two half hitches.

4. Tie the other end of the string through the bottom holes using the method in step 3. Glue the knots and the places where the string crosses the spine at the back. Let the glue dry.

5. Test the kite to make sure it is balanced and make any adjustments (see the tip on page 8).

6. Measure the bridle to find its centre. Tie a ring-pull just above the centre using a lark's head hitch (see page 8).

7. To make the reel and kite line, turn to page 10, or use one you have made already.

4 The tail

This kite flies well either with or without a tail. If you want to add a tail to your birdie, follow these steps.

1. Cut tissue paper or crêpe paper into strips 3cm (1¼in) wide. Glue them together to make three streamers, each measuring 3m (10ft) long.

2. When the glue is dry, crush each streamer into a ball. Gently smooth each one out. Then do the same thing again.

3. Glue 4cm (1½in) at one end of each streamer. Stick the streamers to the base of the birdie's tail. Let the glue dry.

Overlap 4cm (1½in)

⬩5⬩ The bow string

This simple device can be added to the spar of a flat kite. It bends the spar into a gentle bow, so the kite sits in the wind, like a cradle. The wind moves past the kite more smoothly and this makes flying easier.

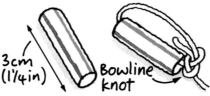

3cm (1¼in)

Bowline knot

1. Cut two 3cm (1¼in) pieces of drinking straw. Thread the end of an 80cm (31½in) piece of string through one straw. Tie the string in a bowline knot as shown on the right.

The bowline

This is what the knot looks like when it is tied below the straw.

Loop the string below the straw as shown on the left. Poke the short end down through the loop.

Bring the short end over the top of the long piece, then up through the loop from behind.

Pull

Pull

Pull both ends of the string to tighten the knot.

1cm (½in)

2. Fold over 1cm (½in) of the straw. Push the short end onto the left end of the spar.

3. Thread the end of the string through the other straw. Fold over 1cm (½in) of the straw. Push it onto the other end of the spar.

4. Stand the kite on the spar's left end. Pull the end of the string down gently as shown above, to make the spar start to bend.

8cm (3in)

5. Pull the end until the string between the straws is about 8cm (3in) from the spar's centre. Ask a friend to check.

6. Hold both pieces of string tightly. Draw a pen mark across them, below the straw. Lift the straw off the spar.

7. Tie the string to the straw with a bowline knot. Tie it so the pen marks are in the middle of the completed knot.

8. Bend the spar and push the straw on to the end again. Now try your kite out before you decorate it (see page 12).

Decoration ideas

The birdie looks really effective either with decoration or without. Try out one of these ideas or work out some designs for yourself.

Tip

It will be easier to decorate the birdie if you take the bow string off first. Put it on again when you are ready to fly your kite.

Make an exotic-looking birdie by sticking on bright paper shapes.

Tip

Look in books about birds for more decoration ideas.

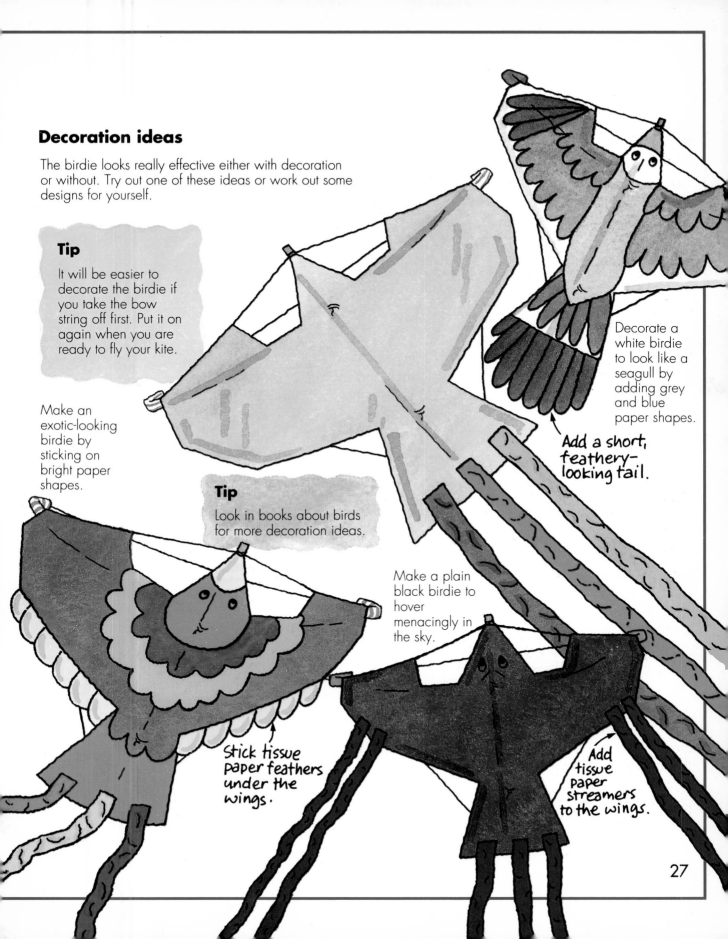

Decorate a white birdie to look like a seagull by adding grey and blue paper shapes.

Add a short, feathery-looking tail.

Make a plain black birdie to hover menacingly in the sky.

Stick tissue paper feathers under the wings.

Add tissue paper streamers to the wings.

Square kite

This kite is made from material. It has a bridle which is fixed to the cover in three places. This is called a three-legged bridle.

Find out how to make a square kite on the next four pages. Fly your finished model in moderate to strong winds.

You will need these things:	Thin cane or dowel (3mm or ⅛in) thick): two 60cm (23½in) pieces and a 16cm (6¼in) piece	A thin needle and thread
Dressmaker's interfacing 49 x 53cm (19½ x 20¾in) (buy medium thickness)	Three ring-pulls	A matchstick
	Thin string	Four pieces of cardboard 4 x 6cm (1½ x 2½in)
	A thick needle	Coloured tissue paper
		Sandpaper

1 Making the cover

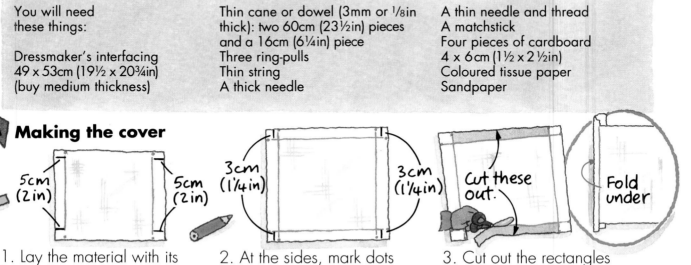

1. Lay the material with its long edges at the top and bottom. Mark these edges with dots 5cm (2in) in from each corner. Use a pencil and ruler to join the dots as shown above.

2. At the sides, mark dots 3cm (1¼in) down from the top corners and 3cm (1¼in) up from the bottom corners. Join the dots as shown above.

3. Cut out the rectangles which are shaded grey in the picture above. Then fold the side strips under along the pencil lines.

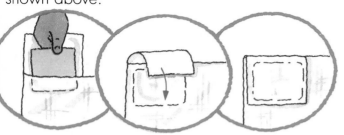

4. Slip one of the small pieces of cardboard into one corner, between the two layers of material. Glue the small flap of material and fold it over to the front. Press it down and let it dry.

5 Glue the other corners as you did in step 4. Only take the cardboard out when the glue is dry.

6. At each corner, sew along the outside edges of the flaps. Use the thin needle and thread.

2 The spars

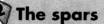

1. Mark the canes or dowel with the measurements shown here. Lay them across the cover from corner to corner, to check that they fit.

15cm (6in)

Make the marks all the way around.

Back of kite

Tip

If the spars stick out, ask an adult to cut a small piece off both ends of each one. Rub the spars smooth with sandpaper.

2. Slip the end of one spar into the cover's left pocket, at the top. Bend the spar and slip the other end into the other pocket, at the bottom.

3. Fit the second spar between the other two corners.

3 The bridle

1. On the cover, make a dot underneath each of the marks which you drew on the spars. Make holes at each dot using the thick needle. Wiggle the needle around to make the hole slightly bigger.

2. Cut two 70cm (27½in) pieces of string. Thread one onto the thick needle.

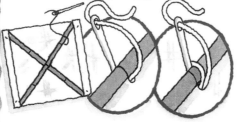

3. With the spars facing upwards, poke the needle up through the top right hole. Take it over the spar and down through the hole. Do this a second time.

4. Turn the kite over and complete the knot. It is a round turn with two half hitches (see page 8, step 4).

Front of kite

5. Now do the same with the other piece of string at the top left hole.

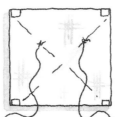

6. Thread one of the pieces of string back onto the needle. Use the method in steps 3 and 4 to attach it through the centre hole and around both spars at the back of the kite, as shown above.

Back of kite

Cross both spars here.

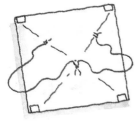

7. Tie the second piece of string through the centre hole, as you did in step 6. See the next tip before you tighten the knot.

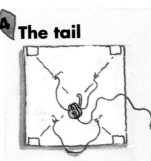

Tip
Measure both pieces of string to make sure they are the same length. Adjust the second piece if necessary.

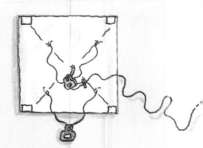

The tail

1. Tie the ends of a 70cm (27½in) piece of string through the lower holes. Use the method in section 3, steps 3 and 4.

2. Measure the string and mark the centre. Tie a ring-pull at the mark using a lark's head hitch (see page 8).

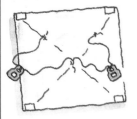

8. Measure and mark the centre of both pieces of string. Tie a ring-pull at each mark with a lark's head hitch (page 8).

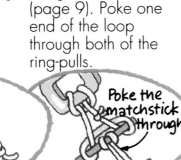

Reef knot

9. Tie the ends of a 30cm (12in) piece of string in a reef knot (page 9). Poke one end of the loop through both of the ring-pulls.

15cm (6in)

3. Cut strips of tissue paper 15cm (6in) wide. Glue them together to make a 6m (19½ft) tail. Let the glue dry.

4. Crush the tail into a ball then smooth it out. Do this a second time.

Pull

Poke the matchstick through.

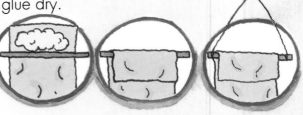

10. Poke the other end of the loop through the first end as shown above. Then pull it tight.

11. Fold the loop over as shown on page 9, step 6. Add the reel and kite line (page 10) as shown above.

5. Glue 5cm (2in) at one end of the tail. Lay the 16cm (6¼in) cane or dowel across as shown above. Fold the paper over.

6. Now tie on a 60cm (23½in) piece of string as shown above. Use round turns with two half hitches (page 8).

Other ideas

Make the cover from brown wrapping paper or pieces of crackly plastic bag taped together. The pieces of plastic must be the same thickness.

Instead of sewing the corners to strengthen them, fold pieces of sticky tape over them as shown here.

Sticky tape

Before you make the holes in the cover, add pieces of sticky tape, so the cover does not tear.

Sticky tape

Decoration ideas

 Painting and colouring

Use poster paints or felt-tip pens to make a face or a flower on your kite.

Potato printing

Cut out potato shapes. Add bright paint to them, then print patterns on the material before you make your kite. You could use two or three different shapes.

Decorate the tail to look like a scarf or a tie.

Add a green tail to look like a stem.

8. Poke the matchstick through the ring-pull at the kite's base.

7. Mark the centre of the string. Tie a matchstick on at the mark using a lark's head hitch (see the pictures in step 6, on page 9).

9. Glue all the knots on the kite. Glue the string where it crosses the spars at the back. Let it dry.

31

Birdie template

Here's how to make the template for the birdie kite. You will need plain paper 50 x 60cm (19½ x 23½in).

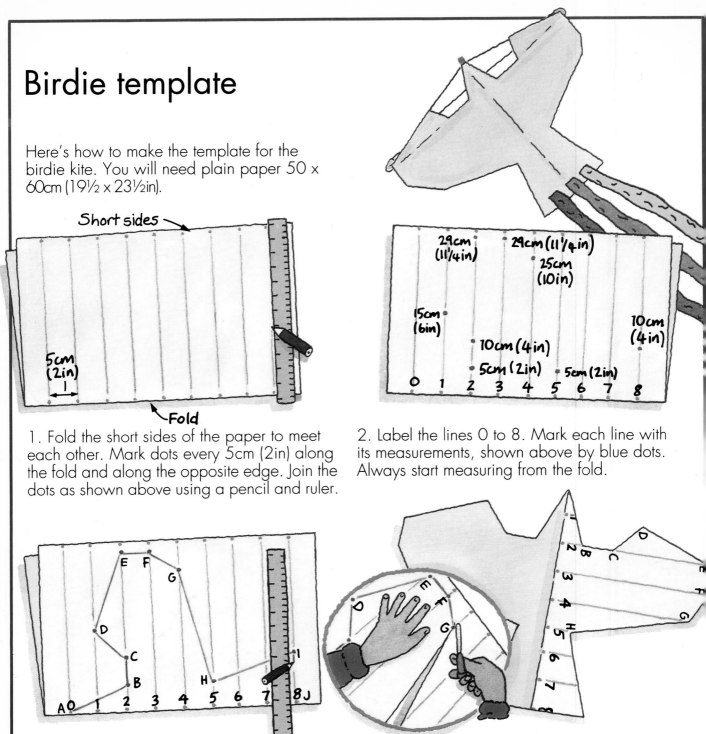

Short sides

Fold

5cm (2in)

1. Fold the short sides of the paper to meet each other. Mark dots every 5cm (2in) along the fold and along the opposite edge. Join the dots as shown above using a pencil and ruler.

29cm (11¼in)   29cm (11¼in)
25cm (10in)
15cm (6in)   10cm (4in)
10cm (4in)
5cm (2in)   5cm (2in)
0 1 2 3 4 5 6 7 8

2. Label the lines 0 to 8. Mark each line with its measurements, shown above by blue dots. Always start measuring from the fold.

3. Look carefully at the picture above and label the points A to J on your paper. Join the points in alphabetical order using a pencil and ruler.

4. Keeping the paper folded, cut along the lines you have just drawn. Then open up the paper to see the completed birdie shape. Now turn back to page 22.

32